1

A GILBERT MORRIS MYSTERY

D1377825

MOODY PRESS
CHICAGO

"TOO SMART" JONES

and the
Pool Party
Thief

1

JONES

Contents

1

Too Smart Is Too Bad

Juliet Jones hurried down the hall. She hurried so fast that she stepped on Tony Dutton's heels.

He turned and said, "Hey! Walk on your own feet, will you? They're big enough!"

"They're no bigger than yours!" Juliet snapped back. That was true. But her feet *were* a little longer than those of other girls her age. Tony had found out she was embarrassed about them. He never missed a chance to tease her.

Melanie Black had been walking with Tony. She was a pretty girl with curly golden hair and blue eyes. She had on a beautiful dark blue dress. "Better get out of her way, Tony," she said. "We wouldn't want to stop Too Smart Jones from getting all her prizes!"

"Don't call me that, Melanie!" Juliet cried.

Melanie had given Juliet the nickname "Too Smart" weeks ago. Now all the other kids in school had started calling her Too Smart—even the ones in other classes. Juliet hated it.

They reached the door to the auditorium. Just as Juliet went through, she said, "Maybe I'll start calling you Too-Dumb Melanie! How would you like that?"

Suddenly Mrs. Barry, the fourth grade teacher, appeared. She had been at the end of the line, but she must have heard the argument. Mrs. Barry's usually kind black eyes were a little stern. "Juliet, you know better than to call anyone dumb," she said quietly.

Juliet liked Mrs. Barry better than any other teacher she'd ever had. But she complained, "She started it. She called me by that awful nickname, Mrs. Barry!"

"And I've already talked to Melanie about that," her teacher said. The class was all inside the large auditorium by then. "We'll talk more about it later. Now all of you take your seats. Quietly."

Juliet walked on down the aisle. It was Awards Day for grades one to four. She had been looking forward to today for weeks. But Melanie and Tony had already spoiled the event for her. She sat down between Matthew Jennings and Debby Simms.

Matthew jammed an elbow into her ribs. He whispered, "Aw, don't be mad, Too Smart.

Think of all them awards you're going to get!"

Juliet saw that Mrs. Barry was watching, so she just clamped her teeth together.

Annie Patterson sat behind her. Annie was a tall, thin girl. She always wore clothes that didn't fit, but she was sweet. Patting Juliet's shoulder, she whispered, "Don't pay any attention to him, Juliet. He's jealous like all the rest of them."

Just then the principal, Mr. Davidson, came to the microphone. "We want to welcome all of our guests to our annual Awards Day. Will all of you who are relatives of one of our students please stand?"

The grown-ups stood. Juliet saw her parents down in the second row. They were looking for her, and she waved until her mother saw her. Her mom pulled at Mr. Jones's sleeve, pointed out Juliet, and then they both waved. Juliet saw her brother, Joe, waving at them, too. He was in third grade.

Then Mr. Davidson said, "We'll start with the first grade. Mrs. Simpson, will you please come and give the awards to our youngest pupils?"

Juliet clapped for all the winners in the first grade.

It took a long time to get through the first three grades. But finally Mr. Davidson said, "Now, the fourth grade. Mrs. Barry will present the awards."

Mrs. Barry went up on the stage. She said, "I think *all* the fourth graders deserve an award."

Right away a boy whispered loudly, "Well, just give us all one then!"

It was Tony Dutton, Juliet knew. Mrs. Barry frowned at him, then began to present the awards. "For the fourth grade spelling award, the winner is Juliet Jones. Juliet, come and get your trophy."

Juliet got out of her seat. Her heart was thumping. As she started down the row to the aisle, Debby pinched her hard. Juliet almost cried out loud. But she knew that was what Debby wanted.

When she got to the stage, Mrs. Barry handed her a little silver cup. "We're all proud of Juliet," she said.

Juliet took the trophy and looked down at her parents. Both of them were smiling. She saw Joe with the third graders. Joe was smiling, too. He was clapping as hard as he could.

Then Mrs. Barry said, "I have asked the fourth grade winners to stay on the stage until all the awards have been given."

Juliet stepped back, and Mrs. Barry went on. "The award for best handwriting goes to Annie Patterson."

As Annie came up onto the stage, Juliet clapped for her. She was wearing an ugly dress, and Juliet felt sorry for her.

But Annie didn't seem to mind. She smiled and said, "Oh, thank you, Mrs. Barry!" She took her place beside Juliet.

Mrs. Barry gave the geography award to Leroy Anderson. Then she said, "Now, this is very unusual, but the rest of the awards go to the same person. The history award, the story-writing award, and the science award all go to—Juliet Jones!"

A stir went around the room. People clapped. But Juliet saw that some of the parents looked upset. *It's not my fault!* she said to herself as she went to take the awards from her teacher. She could hardly hold them all.

Suddenly the spelling trophy fell with a clatter. And then a voice said—loudly enough for everybody to hear—"What's the matter, Too Smart? You got butterfingers?" It was Tony Dutton, of course.

All over the room, boys and girls laughed. Juliet knew her face was red. She picked up the trophy, and all of a sudden tears began to roll down her cheeks!

Mrs. Barry said firmly, "Tony, you will be quiet!" Then she whispered to Juliet, "There, there, Juliet! Don't cry. Tony didn't mean anything by it."

"He did, too!" she sobbed. She had so looked forward to Awards Day, and now it was all spoiled! When the ceremony was over, she stumbled off the stage.

"I'll hold your awards, Juliet," her mother said. "Don't cry. We're all very proud of you."

But Juliet couldn't keep the tears back. She looked across the room. Matthew Jennings was sticking his tongue out at her. Tony Dutton was crossing his eyes and mouthing, "Too Smart! Too Smart!"

"I wish I'd never gotten any of these old awards!" she said angrily. "It's awful to be too smart!"

2

Big News

It was two weeks after Awards Day. Juliet and Joe had just finished the dinner dishes.

Their father said, "Let's go into the den. Your mother and I have some news for you."

"Are we going to get a new TV set?" Joe asked.

"No, it's more exciting than that," Mr. Jones said as he led them out of the kitchen.

"Are you going to get me a playhouse?" Juliet asked as they sat down on the couch.

"No, it's better than that," their father said.

"Nothing could be better than that!" Juliet cried.

"Just listen," Mr. Jones said. "I've been transferred to another town—to Oakwood. We'll be moving in a few weeks."

Juliet looked at him in surprise. Then she said loudly, "Good! Now I won't have to go to that rotten school anymore!"

"The school isn't rotten, dear," her mom said. "You've done very well here, and so has Joe."

"Nobody likes me here," Juliet said. She put a stubborn look on her face. "All the kids are jealous of me because I make good grades."

But her mother said, "Not all of them. Annie Patterson was glad to see you win your awards. And so were some of the others." She looked over at Mr. Jones. "Juliet, your dad and I have tried to warn you about something. I'm not sure you are listening. You're a very bright girl. But you must remember that it was God who made you that way. Sometimes, I'm afraid, you are a little proud of your ability."

"She sure is!" Joe said. "I'm better at basketball than she is, but you don't hear *me* bragging about it."

Juliet was angry. "I can't help it if I'm smart," she said. "I can't make myself *dumb*, can I?"

"Of course not," her father said. "But you'd have more friends if you used the ability God has given you to help others—not just to win prizes for yourself."

Juliet knew that her parents were right. But she didn't want to admit it. "Anyway, the new school will be just as bad as this one!"

"I don't think so," her dad said. He looked as if he'd just thought of a joke. "I hate to tell you this, children, but I'm in love with your new teacher."

Joe and Juliet stared.

Both of their parents laughed.

Then Dad said, "Your mother and I have been praying about your education. And we believe that God wants us to be homeschoolers. So your mother will be your new teacher."

"You mean we won't go to school?" Juliet asked.

"Hooray!" Joe shouted. He got up and did a war dance. "No more dumb old homework!"

"Hold on!" Mr. Jones was smiling, but he was serious too. "You'll go to school all right but not in a school building. And if you think your mother will let you have a party all day, you're going to get a shock."

"We'll work hard," their mother said. "But we'll do it as a family instead of a school classroom."

"But you say you aren't good at arithmetic, Mom!" Juliet said. "How will you teach us if you don't know it?"

"Your father will do that, Juliet," Mrs. Jones said. "And in things like science, we'll get someone from our support group to teach you. Then we'll teach *their* children reading or history."

"What's a support group?" Joe asked.

"It's a group of parents who teach their children at home," Mrs. Jones said. "We'll have a fine one in Oakwood. You'll meet lots of nice boys and girls. And we'll get together often to go on trips and have contests."

"And parties?" Joe wanted to know.

"And parties too. Sometimes!" Then Mrs. Jones came over to the couch and sat between Juliet and Joe. Putting her arms around both of them, she said, "This kind of school is going to be very different. But it will be worth it."

Then Juliet's dad came and sat beside her. He put his arm around her, too. "You've had a hard time at this school, Juliet. But now you can start all over again. And it's going to be wonderful!"

Juliet wasn't so sure.

Joe said, "Know what I think, Dad?"

"What?"

"I think we ought to celebrate our new school. I think we ought to take our new teacher out and buy her a banana split."

"That's a good idea!" their dad said. He got to his feet and pulled the others up off the couch. "I'm glad I thought of it!"

As they went down to the drive-in, Joe kept talking about their new home. But Juliet was thinking, *I'm going to think of something! They're not going to call me Too Smart Jones in our new town!*

3

Juliet's Plan

Juliet stomped into her brother's room. "Joe, you give me my shirt right now!"

He was wearing her new T-shirt with the yellow lion on the front. She tried to pull the shirt off him. "You *know* I wanted to wear it!"

Joe grabbed her hands and grinned at her. "Aw, it looks better on me than it does on you! Besides that, you wore *my* shirt yesterday— and you got it all dirty, too."

"I don't care! You just take it off right now!"

Juliet pulled at the shirt. Joe tripped and fell. He pulled her down with him. The two of them rolled on the floor.

Their mother came to the door and looked at them crossly. "Children! Get up from there! We're going to be late for our first support group meeting!"

"Mom, make him give me my shirt!" Juliet pleaded.

"Joe, you look silly! Give Juliet her shirt. Breakfast is on the table, so hurry up."

Joe pulled the shirt over his head. He handed it to Juliet. "There's your old shirt. It looks better on me, though!"

Juliet went back to her room. She put on her new jeans. Then she pulled the shirt over her head. She had a pair of new Nike shoes and a new barrette for her hair. It was made of small balloons of all colors. Then she heard her mother call.

When she got downstairs, her father grinned at her. "You'll be the prettiest girl in the whole group, Juliet! Now let's eat and get on our way."

As they drove across Oakwood to the meeting, Joe said, "I hope we get the book stuff out of the way fast and get to play ball."

"Well, whatever happens, be polite," Mrs. Jones said. "And remember that some of these parents will be helping you with your schoolwork."

"I don't see why we have to get mixed up with anybody else," Juliet said. "We're doing all right by ourselves. I'm learning more from you than I did from any other teachers, Mom."

"People need each other, Juliet," Mrs. Jones said. "Remember that verse we learned yesterday?"

Juliet remembered. "'Two are better than one because they have a good return for their labor.' That's Ecclesiastes 4:9."

"That's right. And do you remember the next verse, Joe?" Mr. Jones asked.

"Sure. It says if one guy falls, then the other one will help him up. But the one who is by himself when he falls doesn't have anybody to help him."

Juliet said, "Well, *I* don't intend to fall. And I wish we didn't have to get into all this support group stuff!"

"You need friends, Juliet," her father put in. "We all do."

"The kids in our old school wouldn't be friends. They made fun of me because I made the best grades," Juliet said again.

Her father and mother gave each other a strange glance. But Mr. Jones said, "Well, now you have a chance to start over. Try to be a little kinder to the boys and girls who aren't as good as you are in their work."

Juliet just looked at him. But an idea was creeping into her mind. She kept quiet the rest of the way. And by the time they pulled up in front of the small red brick church, she had made her plan.

I don't know why I never thought of this before, she thought as they got out of the van. *All I have to do is just not let people find out I'm good at anything.*

They walked up the steps and went inside.

Juliet nodded to herself. *I guess I can be as dumb as anybody! And if that'll keep kids from calling me Too Smart Jones, it'll be worth it!*

A woman with short blonde hair and a pair of sparkling blue eyes met them. "Hello. I'm Vicki White. You must be the Joneses."

"I'm Mark Jones," Dad said, "and this is my wife, Rachel. And this is Joe and Juliet."

Mrs. White smiled at them all. "I'm so glad to meet you. We're just getting started. This way."

The Joneses followed her down a hall and into a large room. Mrs. White introduced them.

A big man was standing in front of the parents and children. "I'm Harold Rollins, folks. This is my wife, Louise. And this is my son Billy, here." Then he said, "We'll let the children go out and play while we have our meeting."

Mr. Rollins was a bossy kind of man, Juliet thought. He was like a police officer directing traffic.

Mrs. White said, "I think it might be good if they listened for a while."

But Mr. Rollins just laughed and waved his hand. "Now, Vicki, you just have a seat and let the children have a good time. Billy, get the volleyball and take the kids out to play."

"Sure, Dad," Billy said. "You kids, come on." He was a large boy, who looked like his father. He was just about as bossy.

Juliet didn't want to go, but she had no choice. She and Joe left the room with the others. On the way down the hall, a small girl with red hair said, "Hello, Juliet. I'm Jenny White. I'm glad you and your brother are going to be in our group."

Juliet liked Jenny at once. Then she thought about her plan. "Well, I don't do too well with books," she said. "As a matter of fact, I'm just plain dumb."

Jenny patted her arm. "Oh, that's all right."

But Billy Rollins turned around to frown at Juliet. He said, "Well, *that's* a pain in the neck! You won't be much good to us at the Home School Bowl, then!"

A boy and a girl who looked alike were watching. They both had brown hair and brown eyes. They wore expensive clothes.

"This is Helen and Ray Boyd, Juliet," Jenny said. "They're twins."

"What about you?" Ray Boyd asked Joe. "Are you dumb, too?"

Joe turned red. "You'll have to wait and find out about that!" he said. "And don't call my sister names!"

Helen Boyd laughed at him. "Well, *she's* the one who said she was dumb. I guess she knows if she's dumb or not."

Joe was getting very angry. "She didn't say she was *dumb*. She said she wasn't good at

21

books." Then he glared at Juliet. "What do you mean telling them—"

Juliet knew what he was about to say. She said quickly, "Oh, I'll do the best I can. That's all anybody can do." She gave Joe a wink. Then she said, "What's this Home School Bowl, Billy?"

Billy Rollins scowled again. "You won't be interested. Not if you're no good at books. Let's go play volleyball."

As they went outside, Joe whispered, "Juliet, what's the idea telling them you're not good at books?"

"Tell you later, Joe," she said. "It's a plan of mine."

For the next hour they played games with the volleyball. Juliet had a good time. The only problem was with Billy Rollins. He kept running over the smaller children. Once he crashed into Jenny White and knocked her to the ground.

"You've got to learn to keep out of the way, Jenny," he said, grinning.

Juliet helped Jenny up. "You skinned your knee. We'd better go put a Band-Aid on it."

"Oh, it's all right." But there were tears in Jenny's eyes.

"I'll go with you," Juliet said. She pulled the smaller girl along. And she ignored Billy Rollins and Ray Boyd, who were yelling at them to stay. "Let's get your mother. I'll bet she knows where the Band-Aids are." She took Jenny inside.

Juliet stuck her head around the meeting-room door. Mr. Rollins was still talking. But Mrs. White saw her, and Juliet motioned for her to come out.

"What's wrong?" Jenny's mother asked.

"Jenny skinned her knee. It needs a Band-Aid."

"Let me see, Jenny." Mrs. White looked and said, "Yes, we need to put something on that. Come this way."

They followed her up the hall.

Soon she had put some medicine on the scrape. As she put on the Band-Aid, she asked, "How did you hurt your knee?"

Jenny didn't answer, but Juliet said, "It was Billy Rollins, Mrs. White. He plays too rough."

Mrs. White nodded. "I've warned him about that. Well, you two go back outside, and we'll see."

The two girls returned to the playground. Right away Juliet saw that all the children were gathered in a circle. And they were shouting.

"Let's see what's wrong, Jenny!" She ran across the yard and looked over the heads of the shorter children. There on the ground was Billy Rollins—on his back. And Joe was on top of him, hitting as hard as he could.

Juliet gave a scream. She pushed through to the boys. "Joe Jones!" she cried. "Stop that!"

But Joe was too angry to listen. He kept yelling, "I told you not to run over that little girl!"

The two boys rolled over and over. Now Billy was yelling, too.

Juliet finally got hold of Joe's arm. She tried to pull him off. "Stop it, Joe!"

And then a big voice thundered, "What's going on here?"

Juliet looked around. It was Mr. Rollins. All the parents were coming out onto the playground.

Mr. Rollins had an angry look on his face. He pulled Joe off Billy. "We don't allow fights here!"

"He started it, Dad!" Billy Rollins's face was dirty. He pointed at Joe. "I wasn't doing a thing. He just came up and hit me!"

Mr. Rollins grabbed Joe's arm. "You've got to learn some manners, young man!"

Then Joe and Juliet's dad stepped up. He took Mr. Rollins's hand off Joe, saying, "We'd better hear both sides of this."

But it was impossible to hear both sides. Billy Rollins kept saying he hadn't done a thing. The Boyd twins agreed with him. A little girl about seven years old tried to speak. But Mr. Rollins wouldn't listen. He said loudly, "Well, we might as well go home. Come along, Billy."

As they left, Juliet's father said, "Sorry about all this, folks."

Mrs. White said quietly, "It's happened before, Mr. Jones."

"I just hope Mr. Rollins doesn't pull out of the support group." The speaker was the mother of the Boyd twins. "He has a lot of influence in this town."

Juliet looked around. Some of the parents didn't seem to be worried about what Mr. Rollins did.

As people were going to their cars, Mrs. White said to Juliet, "Thanks for looking out for Jenny. That was sweet." Then she stopped smiling. "Since her father died, she hasn't been doing so well. I hope the two of you can be friends."

"Oh, we will be, Mrs. White!"

On the way home, Joe was still angry. He said, "It just made me mad—the way Billy Rollins pushed the little kids around!" Then he looked at his dad. "Are you mad at me?"

"No, Son, I'm not mad. But in the future try to use a little restraint. That means keep your temper under control."

As soon as Juliet and Joe were alone, Joe said, "Use a little restraint! The next time, I'll use a brickbat on that guy!" Then he asked again, "What did you mean telling everybody you're not good at books?"

"It's what I'm going to do, Joe." She explained her plan to him. "I'm not going to let

25

anybody know I'm smart. And you can't tell anybody! Promise?"

"I guess so," he muttered. "But it sounds kind of dishonest."

"It's not," Juliet said. "It's just a way of keeping people from making fun of me."

That night, before she went to sleep, Juliet did feel a little guilty. But then she thought, *It's the only way I can keep people from hurting me. It's sort of a protection. God made those little lizards—chameleons. They can change their color to protect themselves. I guess I'm as good as an old lizard!*

She dropped off to sleep, but she had bad dreams about lizards. She dreamed that she was changed to bright purple.

4

Amos

Juliet looked across at Joe.

He was slumped at his desk. He was gnawing the eraser on his pencil. He squinted at the wrinkled paper in front of him. He looked up at her and said, "I can't do this problem! It would take a genius to figure it out!"

Juliet got up from her chair and looked at Joe's paper. She frowned. "I don't see how you can even *read* what you've written. If you'd do neater work, you'd be able to see what you're doing."

She leaned over and wrote down a number on his paper.

"How'd you come up with that?" he demanded. "Mom's going to want to know how I did it."

"I'll show you." Juliet sat down. She started to go over the problem with him.

She liked their study room. Actually it was a carport that had been made a part of the house. The walls were light blue. Sunlight came in through a large picture window in the front. At the back was the long table they used for a workbench. On it was a microscope, a half-finished model airplane that Joe was building, Juliet's collection of old bottles, and bits and pieces of other collections.

To the right of the workbench was a large bookcase. It was made of rough lumber and old concrete blocks. It held all sorts of books—Bible stories, encyclopedias, storybooks, old magazines, even some cartoon books that Joe thought were funny.

"This is a great way to study, isn't it?" she said. "I like it lots better than studying back at school."

"I guess so." But Joe frowned. He put down a number. Then he looked up with a grin. "Now, I've got it! I worked this one all by myself."

Juliet looked at it. "See how easy it is?"

Just then their mother came in.

"Look, Mom, Joe's learned how to do to-day's story problems. And I finished my book report."

"Good work, Joe," Mrs. Jones said. "Let me look over your report, Juliet."

Juliet handed it to her, and her mother sat down and began to read. It was a report on *The Lion, the Witch and the Wardrobe,* by C. S.

Lewis. When she finished, she said, "This is good. But I don't think you've said enough about what the book *means*."

"But I told everything that happened in the story, Mom!"

"Yes, but good writers mean more than they say." Her mother smiled. "Even in the Bible, the stories mean more than they say. For example, we like to read how David won his fight with the giant Goliath, don't we?"

"Sure, Mom," Joe piped up. "That's a great story!"

"But when David won his battle, didn't that show us something more than just his winning?"

Juliet nodded slowly. "Yes. It shows us that God can help us do things."

"Sure," Joe added.

Juliet said, "I think I see what you mean about this book." She thought hard. "There's a lion in it—but it's *more* than just a story about an ordinary lion. I mean, this lion had to die for people—just like Jesus did!"

"That's right. And that kind of story is what we call an *allegory*. That's when a story has another meaning all the way through."

"Like *Pilgrim's Progress?*" Joe asked.

"Yes," she said. "Like *Pilgrim's Progress.*" She handed the paper back to Juliet. "You might want to read the book again. Now that you know what to look for, you'll see something new in it. But right now, it's time for us to go."

"Oh, Mom, I don't want to go to another meeting!" Juliet complained. "We're doing fine without that old support group!"

"Let's go," Mrs. Jones said firmly. "You need time alone with your studies, but you need time with other kids too."

They went through the kitchen and picked up the refreshments they were taking. Soon the three of them were driving to the church.

"If that Billy Rollins gives me any trouble, he'll be sorry!" Joe said as they pulled into the parking lot.

"Try to be nice to him," his mother said. As they took the sandwiches and Kool-Aid out of the van, she said, "I feel sorry for him."

Juliet stared at her. "Why do you feel sorry for Billy Rollins? I feel sorry for all the people who have to put up with him. He's a pain in the neck!"

"Billy isn't a happy boy," Mrs. Jones said. "He bullies people. And there's no such thing as a happy bully."

"He must get it from his dad," Joe said. "He's the bossiest man I ever saw!"

They found Mrs. White in the meeting hall. She turned to them with a smile. "Hello, Rachel."

"Hello, Vicki," Mrs. Jones said. She looked around the room. Boys and girls were playing every sort of game. "Are you sure you don't want me to stay and help you with the children today?"

"Oh, we'll be all right," Mrs. White said. "You did your part bringing refreshments. We ought to be finished by four o'clock."

Juliet and Joe's mom left, and Mrs. White walked to the center of the room. "All right, everyone," she called. "Let's get started." Most of them didn't hear her. She tried again. "Time to get started!" But they still didn't hear.

Juliet pulled at Mrs. White's sleeve. "I can make them listen," she said. She put two fingers in her mouth and gave her loudest whistle.

All the noise stopped. All the boys and girls stared at Juliet.

"Well, that's one way to get attention," Mrs. White said and laughed. "You'll have to be our official whistler, Juliet." Then she said, "Let's all sit down. And we'll make our plans to win the Home School Bowl."

Juliet and Joe sat together on the floor. Jenny White came and sat with them. "Hello, Juliet," she said.

"Hello, Jenny." Then Juliet asked, "What's the Home School Bowl?"

Mrs. White overheard the question. "For those of you who are new," she said, "let me explain the Home School Bowl. You all know about the Super Bowl. It's where the two best football teams play each other. Well, once a year, we have a question-and-answer Super Bowl with the Cedar City homeschoolers. So far, we've never won. Cedar City has a larger group, so they have more children to choose from."

"I'm tired of losing to them!" Helen Boyd snapped. "If we lose this year, I'm going to quit!"

Her brother Ray said, "We need some smart kids to beat them. That's what we need."

"Well, I don't see any *new* smart kids here." Billy Rollins was looking at Juliet and Joe. "From what I hear, the new ones we got won't do us any good."

"Billy!" Mrs. White said sharply. Then she said, "We'll begin by asking God to help our team get ready."

After the prayer, Mrs. White said, "Now, what we'll do today is see what our strong points are. And our weaknesses. All of you are better at some things than you are at others. First, we'll see who are the best spellers. Let's try an old-fashioned spelling bee."

Juliet had always liked spelling bees.

As they lined up, Joe whispered, "This would be a good time to forget about being dumb."

She shook her head.

Mrs. White began giving out words. She started with easy ones such as "dog" and "bone." Then they got harder.

Juliet saw at once that Helen and Ray Boyd were good spellers. So were Jenny and nine-year-old Mitch Dubois. Then some of the younger children started to miss words.

Juliet didn't want to appear *too* dumb. She waited until Mrs. White gave her the word "automatic." She spelled it wrong on purpose.

"Good night!" Ray Boyd said in disgust. "What a fat lot of help *she's* going to be!"

The spelling bee went on until everyone was out except the Boyd Twins.

Mrs. White said, "There's time for all of you to improve. Now, then, let's see who does well with addition."

They lined up again. This time Juliet stayed in line longer. *I don't want to be called Too-Dumb Jones, she thought. That would be as bad as Too Smart Jones!*

They worked on addition drill for about five minutes. Ray Boyd seemed very good at numbers.

Then the door opened, and a boy came in.

Billy Rollins muttered, "Well, here's Amos the Turtle—late as usual."

Amos was larger than any other boy in the room. He wore a pair of jeans that were too big for him. He had on a blue shirt, also too big. On his feet were tennis shoes that had once been white. On his head was a blue base-ball cap with the bill pointed sideways. He had a round face and sandy hair.

"Come in, Amos," Mrs. White said. "You're just in time for addition practice." She added, "This is Amos Redfield. Amos, you haven't met Juliet and Joe Jones. They're new in town."

Amos gave them a look, then ducked his head and muttered something. Juliet couldn't understand a word he said.

She heard Ray Boyd mumble, "We'll be all right in the Home School Bowl now. We've got Amos and his mighty brain to see us through!"

"That's quite enough, Ray," Mrs. White said firmly. "Amos, why don't you stand beside Mary Rose and Lyle?"

The large boy shuffled over to stand in line. As the drill went on, he kept looking down at the floor. Once he lifted his head and looked right at Juliet. Then he got red and dropped his head again. When Mrs. White gave him a simple addition problem, he mumbled the answer. But the problems got harder. On the next one, he just shook his head. He left the line and sat down by himself.

Mrs. White made them practice for two hours. Juliet knew quite a bit more about the boys and girls by then. She knew that Lyle Turner was best at history. Pearl Keeler knew geography better than anyone else. Roy Keeler was good at both math and science. Mitch Dubois seemed to be good in every subject.

Others, Juliet saw, were not very good at anything—especially Martin Dubois and Amos

Redfield. And she knew that the rest of the boys and girls had put her on the level of Martin and Amos.

She had managed to give wrong answers to questions in every subject. The Boyd twins were disgusted with her. They complained that she would be no help in the Home School Bowl. Others—like Jenny—seemed to feel sorry for her. And Joe just stared at her and shook his head.

At going home time, Mrs. White said, "We all need to work hard. No matter how well you can do, you'll be competing against students who are smart. You know the Bible says, 'Whatever your hand finds to do, do it with all your might.' Now, I'm your coach, but I can't win the contest for you. But I know a secret. I know how you can help your team be its best in the Home School Bowl."

"What's the secret?" Joe asked.

"It's easy," Mrs. Jones said. "Just think how you can help your friends do better. Let's be just like a family. Try to help each other get ready. And that will help *you*." Then she said, "I'm going to write down some instructions for each of you to take home. But while I do that, you can start on the refreshments Mrs. Jones brought."

A yell went up.

"Pearl," Mrs. White said, "you and Josie be the hostesses today. There's plenty. Just see that everyone takes turns."

"You mean why she still isn't doing better?" Mrs. Jones said. "I really don't know. She's always done so well with schoolwork in the past. We just can't understand why she's doing so poorly with the team."

"I've looked over her work," Mrs. White said. "She does great work at home. But as soon as she gets with the other children, she just seems . . . different."

"Maybe she just hasn't gotten used to the idea yet. But I know you'll pull her out of it. You're one of the best teachers I ever saw."

Mrs. Jones patted her shoulder. "Don't worry," she said. "It's not you. The children are learning. You're doing a fine job."

Then she heard the three youngsters coming down the stairs. "I'm glad you're taking the kids with you. It'll be good for them."

For the next two hours, Juliet and Joe had a fine time with Jenny and her mother. They even stopped for snacks—twice! And everywhere they went to deliver school materials, the other children wanted to go with them.

"I should have brought a bus!" Mrs. White joked.

The Boyds were a little stiff. "I don't really think Ray and Helen need these books," Mrs. Boyd said. "But thank you, anyway."

Mrs. Rollins took the books and said, "Thank

you." But she looked at Juliet and Joe with an angry expression.

"I don't think she likes us much," Juliet said after they left.

"Billy's probably told them all sorts of things about us," Joe said. "Ever since our fight, he's been really mean."

"He'll come around," Mrs. White said. "Now, one more stop." She drove out of town and turned the car down a dirt road. The dust rose in the air as they rolled along. Out in the fields were white-faced cows that looked curiously at them. Most of the cows had small wobbly-legged calves beside them.

Finally they came to a house set way back off the road. "Who lives here?" Joe asked. "It looks like a haunted house!"

"This is where the Redfields live." Mrs. White slowed down. "Now, don't be surprised if Amos's parents are a little strange."

Was there some mystery at the Redfield house? Juliet wondered right away. She liked mysteries. "They never come to the support meetings," she said.

"No, and I wish they would. They like the idea of homeschooling the children, though." Mrs. White stopped the car. "Now just don't be surprised at anything you see."

As soon as Juliet got out, something banged against her leg. She looked down and saw that it was a small goat! It butted her again.

"Must be the watch goat," her brother said.

Juliet pushed the goat away and looked around. Chickens were pecking at the ground everywhere. Three large peacocks with beautiful tails were stepping carefully around the front yard. Two large dogs and a family of black-and-tan puppies were lying on the porch.

"Be careful," Mrs. White said. "The steps are a little shaky."

Despite her warning, Juliet almost fell through. A board suddenly gave way beneath her foot.

Joe grabbed her arm and pulled her up. "You're supposed to be *dumb*, not clumsy!" he whispered.

Then the front door opened, and children started coming out. There were five of them—three girls and two boys. Three were very young. Amos was the largest. The older girl looked exactly like him, though she wasn't as big. Amos and his brother and sisters stood looking at their visitors.

Mrs. White said, "Hello, Amos. Are your parents home?"

Amos said slowly, "Mom—she's—here."

At these words, a woman came to the door. She was a small lady with reddish hair tied up in a bun. She was wiping her hands on an apron. She said, "Oh, it's you."

"You remember me, Mrs. Redfield," Mrs.

White said. "I was here last month. We came by today to bring Amos some books."

Mrs. Redfield said, "Why, thank you!" She took the books and rubbed them with her hand. "I'm so glad to have these."

"Have you thought more about coming to the group meetings?"

The woman suddenly looked uncomfortable. "I'd like to, but it's hard with all my work. And the truck quit running last week. So we have to walk. And . . ."

Mrs. White said, "Well, you do the best you can, Mrs. Redfield. And the rest of us will try to help more. Debby Dubois tells me she's been coming by to help Amos with arithmetic."

"She surely has." The woman nodded. "And if she hadn't come, I don't know what we'd have done."

"Is your husband home?" Mrs. White asked then. "I've never met him."

"He's not feeling too well," Mrs. Redfield said.

"Some other time, then." Mrs. White turned to go, and Juliet and Joe and Jenny followed her.

As Mrs. White turned the car around, Juliet looked back. All five Redfield children were standing on the porch watching them go. She waved. The children just stared. Then suddenly Amos lifted his hand and gave a small wave.

"What a drag!" Joe said. "They aren't very

friendly, are they? What's wrong with Mr. Red-field, anyway?"

"Nobody really knows." Mrs. White glanced into the rearview mirror. "You can tell that Mrs. Redfield is an educated lady. But Mr. Redfield—I don't know anything about him. You hear all kinds of rumors about him. Some say he's a criminal who is hiding out! A few months back a story got started that he is mentally ill."

"Boy!" Joe said. "*That's* not so good!"

Maybe there *was* a mystery here. "The kids looked sort of scared," she said.

"They don't see many people," Mrs. White said. "They keep to themselves." Then she was quiet for a long time.

Juliet kept thinking about the family in the mysterious old house.

Finally Mrs. White said, "I don't think the children do much but study and work. Look at Amos's hands sometimes. They're hard and rough from hard work."

"His mother's too," Juliet said. She looked down at her own hands. They were soft and white. "I don't think I would like that," she said slowly.

"Amos doesn't have any choice," Mrs. White said. "None of them do."

All the way back to town, Juliet thought of the old house and unhappy Mrs. Redfield. She thought of Amos and how he'd waved at her.

She suddenly thought, *I'll bet Amos isn't dumb like they all say he is. I'll bet he's just scared!*

By the time they got back home, she was thinking of ways to help Amos. As a matter of fact, she got so busy thinking about Amos that for a while she forgot all about herself.

6

The Party

By the end of the month, hot weather had come to Oakwood. The Joneses were not used to it. Juliet and Joe complained a lot. But they spent a lot of time in the small swimming pool in their backyard. Nothing felt better than plunging into cool water in the heat of the day.

One Monday Mrs. Jones said at breakfast, "I think it's time we asked your Home School Bowl team and their parents over for a party. Would you like that?"

"Yes!" Juliet said quickly.

"It'll be a little crowded," her father said. "But I think we can squeeze them all in."

On the following Saturday at three o'clock, the first guests began arriving. Mrs. White and Jenny came first. Right behind them came the Keelers. Mr. and Mrs. Keeler had black hair and dark eyes, and the children all had the same. Their two boys were Tim and Roy. Pearl and Josie were the girls.

The Turners came a little later. Their daughter Lynn was eight, and Mary Rose was ten. Lyle was thirteen, and Jack was nine.

The Dubois family brought their three: Dani, Mitch, and Martin.

The Boyds and the Rollinses came in the same car. "Sorry to be late," Mr. Rollins said. "I couldn't get away from the office." Ray and Helen were dressed in new clothes. So was Billy.

"You didn't have to dress up," Mrs. Jones told them. "I expect you'll get all hot and sweaty."

"Oh, that's all right," Mrs. Boyd said quickly. "We brought a change of clothes for them."

"The badminton net is set up. And the basketball goal," Mr. Jones said. "The swimming pool's out back, too. You'll have to take turns there, though. It's rather small."

"Next time, we'll have the party at our house," Mr. Rollins said. "We have a big pool."

Juliet's mother said, "Juliet, you take the girls to your room to change into swimsuits. The boys can go with Joe."

Soon all were all outside in their swimsuits. Some were already in the water. Juliet and Helen were standing beside the pool.

"Look what I got for my birthday," Helen said. "A camera. And I have two rolls of film."

"Hey, that's neat!" Joe posed on the pool ladder. "You can start by taking a picture of the best-looking boy at this party."

Jack Turner gave him a shove. Joe waved his arms, then fell into the pool with a great splash. "Now," Jack said, "you can have the *really* best-looking guy in your picture!"

But then Billy Rollins gave Jack a shove, yelling, "Never mind them, Helen! Get *my* picture!"

By that time, all the boys were hollering and trying to get on the ladder.

Helen said, "I think you're all terrible." She aimed the camera at her brother. "I'll take your picture first, Ray."

"Aw, you can take his picture anytime," Josie Keeler said. She put her arm around Juliet. "Get a picture of Juliet and me."

Helen frowned. But when Josie said, "Come on, Helen. Take our picture, or I'll throw you into the pool," she took a picture of them.

Some of the smaller children played croquet. Juliet was helping little Tim Keeler hit the ball when someone said, "Amos and his sister are here!"

"What a drag!" Billy Rollins muttered. "He's too dirty to get into the pool with us!"

But Juliet ran to meet them. "Amos, I'm so glad you've come," she said. "And you too, June." She saw that the girl was very shy.

What do you think, Vicki? You've been around Amos more than the rest of us."

Mrs. White had a troubled look on her face. "Amos is so afraid of people that there's no way to really know him. I've been praying for a way to be a friend to him. But it's hard to know how." She looked outside. "Maybe what we're seeing out there is the best way. If the children will just be good to them, I think they'll come around."

"Vicki," Mrs. Jones said, "let's set out the refreshments for the kids."

They went to the kitchen, and soon the tables in the yard were loaded with plates of cookies, bags of chips, and bowls of ice cream. For the next few minutes, it was almost quiet as the children gobbled down the food like hungry lions.

"We may have to go to the store again," Juliet's mother said, grinning. "Haven't any of you had a meal lately?"

"This is great, Mrs. Jones!" Josie called out. "Can I have some more cake? It's the best I ever had!"

"Every piece of cake you have is the best you ever had, Josie." Juliet handed the girl another slice. Then she said, "Here, June, have some cake before these pigs eat it all!"

"Who's a pig?" Lyle Turner demanded. "Have you seen how much ice cream that brother of yours has put down?"

After a while, Juliet was able to get even June to say a few words. What she said was, "I never was to a party before. I didn't want to come. But Amos made me."

"I'm glad he did," Juliet told her. "I want you to come to our team meetings too."

"I'm not smart enough," June protested softly.

"I'll help you," Juliet said. She winked at Amos, who was sitting next to his sister. "You'll bring her, won't you, Amos?"

He blushed, then said slowly, "Try—to." He seemed to struggle for words. "It's been—the best—time I ever—had."

It was also one of the longest speeches Juliet had ever heard him make. She was happy. "We'll have more parties, Amos. I'm so glad you came."

He got up suddenly. "Got to—go," he said. "It's a—long walk."

"Oh, did you walk? You can't walk home! Not all that way!" Juliet cried.

Amos smiled suddenly. The smile almost made him nice looking. "Can't get there—no other way. Never could—fly so good!"

"The Turners said they're going soon," Juliet said. "They live in the same direction as your house. You wait right here!"

Juliet ran inside and said, "Mr. Turner, could you take Amos and June home when you go? They walked all the way here!"

"All that way?" Mr. Turner said. "Oh, I suppose we can take them. Are you about ready to go?" he asked his wife.

Mrs. Jones gave Amos and June two grocery sacks. "Can't let all this food go to waste," she said. "I'll bet your little brother and sisters will like it."

Amos stared at the bags of food, then said, almost clearly, "Thank you—Mrs. Jones." He took his sister by the hand, and the two left with the Turners.

The Boyds and the Rollinses were the last to leave. It took Ray and Helen a long time to get all their things together. When they were finally at the door, Helen cried, "Wait! I forgot my camera. It's out by the pool!"

"Well, hurry up, Helen," her father said.

She rushed off but was back in a few minutes. "It's gone!" she wailed. "I put it down right on the table. Now it's not there."

"Oh, it's got to be!" her mother said. "Let me help you look." The two went off, but soon they were back. "It's not in the backyard," Mrs. Boyd said. "Not anywhere."

"Someone must have brought it into the house," Juliet's mother said. "Juliet, Joe, look in your rooms. We'll look around down here."

Everyone searched everywhere. No one could find the camera.

Helen began to cry. "Somebody took it!"

Mr. Rollins said, "That boy Amos. He went into the backyard before they left."

"Just to get his cap," Juliet said quickly.

"And he was carrying those big paper sacks," Mr. Rollins said. "*He* took the camera."

"That was just leftover cake and sandwiches in the bags," Juliet's mother protested. "I filled those sacks myself."

"All he had to do was pick up the camera and put it in a sack," Mrs. Boyd said.

"I told you they weren't trustworthy kids!" Mr. Rollins said. "I think we'd better call the police. That camera is gone, and it's probably with Amos Redfield right now!"

"Now wait," Mr. Jones said. "Wait. In the first place, it may just be misplaced. In the second place, if someone did take it, it may not have been Amos at all."

"I hope you don't think any of *our* children would do such a thing!" Mrs. Rollins sniffed. "We're not that sort."

"I think it would be best not to do anything right now," Mr. Jones said. "We don't want to wrongly accuse anyone."

The Boyds and the Rollinses left, grumbling.

As soon as they were gone, Juliet burst out, "I don't care *what* they say! Amos wouldn't steal anything!"

Mr. Jones rubbed his chin. "I hope not, Juliet. But you must remember, Amos may not

have been taught about things like that. Still
. . . if he did take the camera, he needs help.
Not a visit from the police."

"It's time to pray," Mrs. Jones said. "We
need God's help."

They all knelt at the couch. When it was
her turn, Juliet prayed hard for Amos and
June. And when they finished praying, she
said, "I don't think God is going to let us
down."

Her mother smiled. "Jesus never let anyone
down. He'll take care of Amos."

7

Lost in the Woods

Joe, I don't think we ought to go this way."
Juliet looked around at the huge trees that lined the road. They were very old trees. What looked like bundles of straw hung from the branches. The road they were on wound like a snake through them.

"Oh, for crying out loud, Juliet!" her brother snapped. "If we're going to learn how to survive in the wilderness, we've got to get out of the backyard!"

They had left the house at noon, carrying their fishing poles. Now it was after two o'clock. "We didn't tell Mom we were coming this way," Juliet said. "We told her we'd be over by the old school."

"That's not a wilderness!" Joe said crossly. "But if you want to go home, nobody's stopping you!"

Juliet looked at the narrow, winding road. She shook her head. "I'll stay with you. But we've got to be home before supper."

"We'll be home soon enough," he said. Then he stopped and pointed. "There's a creek over there. Maybe we can catch a fish and cook it!"

He left the road, and Juliet followed him through the high grass. "I hope there are no snakes around here," she said nervously.

"Oh, that won't matter." Joe grinned. "I've been reading about how to take care of somebody with snakebite. The first thing you do is take a sharp knife and cut Xs over each fang mark and—"

"I don't want to hear it!" Juliet said quickly. She was glad when they got to the bank of the small brook. It was so pretty—clear and running over smooth stones. "Let's take off our shoes and go wading."

"Not me," Joe said. "I'm going fishing!"

Juliet took off her shoes and socks. The water was cool on her feet. The day was hot. She washed her face in the cool water. Then, while Joe fished, she wandered up and down the little brook. When she finally came back, she found that he had caught two fish.

"Look at these!" he said proudly. "Now we can have a real wilderness meal!"

"We'd better take them home," Juliet said.

"No, I'm going to build a fire and cook

them here." Joe looked around. "I don't see any dry wood. Let's go over that way. Maybe we'll find an old dead tree."

He led the way. Soon they were out of sight of the creek. And there were no paths in these thick woods.

Juliet said, "Joe, let's go back."

"There's a dead tree right there. Plenty of firewood." He began breaking up small sticks. "Come on, Juliet," he said. "Help me get some firewood."

They got a little fire started in a clearing. Then Joe tried to clean the fish. "Dad showed me how," he said. He held them up for her to admire. "Now we need two sticks to put them on."

They were soon holding the fish over the flame. When they turned black, Juliet said, "You can have mine. They look awful!"

"You're a sissy!" At that moment both fish fell off the sticks into the fire. He stood up and said, "We need a frying pan. Next time I'll bring one."

"Joe, let's just go home," Juliet begged. "It's getting late, and I'm tired."

"Oh, all right!" he growled. "We have to put the fire out. Wouldn't want to start a forest fire." He used the water in his canteen to do that. Then he said, "So, come on."

They walked for a few minutes. Suddenly Joe said, "I don't remember passing that big tree . . ."

Juliet looked at the huge twisty oak. "I don't, either. I think we turned the wrong way."

"Then, let's go back to where we cooked the fish and start over. It won't be hard to find the creek. Then we can get back to the road."

They turned around and started back. The thistles and burrs scratched Juliet's legs. She felt like crying. But she didn't want her younger brother to see her.

She said, "We've come a long way. Wasn't the fire about here?"

Joe had a worried look on his face now. "I—I thought it was right here. But I don't see the place."

Juliet began to grow afraid. "We're not lost, are we, Joe?"

"No, of course not!" he said quickly. "I'm just a little mixed up is all." He looked around. He took a deep breath. "That way is north. I can tell by the sun. If we go to our right, we ought to cross the road."

Juliet and Joe were crossing an open field. Here the grass and weeds grew taller than before. Soon they came up to the line of pine trees on the other side.

"We just have to go through these trees," Joe said. "I bet the creek is right over there!"

"I hope so." By now Juliet was really scared. But she didn't want to admit it.

Into the trees they went. The tall pines cut off the sunlight. It was cooler under them, but it was scary too. It was also very quiet. One time a bird of some kind made a loud cry that made them both jump.

"What was that?" Joe asked.

"I don't know, but let's get out of here," Juliet said quickly.

They hurried on. The woods seemed endless. They stumbled over roots. Briars scratched Juliet's face. Her mouth was dry. "I wish we had some water," she said.

"We'll get to the creek soon," Joe promised. "We can get a drink then."

On and on they went into the woods. But they didn't find the creek. Now it was getting darker.

"Joe, let's go *back!*" Juliet whispered. "I'm scared!"

Her brother looked around at the tall, silent trees. "I—think we're lost," he said. Juliet saw that his face was pale. "I don't know how to get back."

Juliet stared at him. Then she said, "Maybe we ought to just go on. These woods have to end *somewhere!*"

"You're right," Joe said. "Let's go, then."

They hurried on through the trees. But the woods kept right on going.

Finally, tears gathered in Juliet's eyes. "Joe, I'm so tired. And I'm really scared. Are you?"

Joe swallowed, then nodded. "I'm just about as scared as I've ever been."

just hide every time someone says something bad about you."

"If you don't come," Joe threatened, "I'll come to get you! I'll drag you there!"

He was only half Amos's size, so that sounded funny. They were all laughing when they got to the bottom of the stairs.

"We'll pick up Amos and June for the next meeting," Mr. Jones was saying. "And don't forget about coming to church as soon as you can."

As her dad drove the van out of the yard, Juliet said, "Daddy, they're nice, aren't they? Not at all like people say."

"They are fine people." Her father was steering carefully to keep on the narrow, winding road. "What they need is some Christian love and care."

"What will Mr. Rollins say if they start coming to the school meetings?"

Joe blurted out, "I don't give a dead rat what he says!"

"Joe!" his mother said.

"Well, all right. But I hope they come. And it'd do Mr. Rollins good to find out he's wrong. Billy too!"

9

Field Trips

The time came closer for the Home School Bowl. Now the Oakwood team met more often to practice. Mrs. White worked long hours. Sometimes everybody left the meeting so tired they could hardly walk.

Still, there was always time for games and field trips. One afternoon Mrs. White took the boys and girls to a meat-packing plant. The people there packaged chickens for sale in stores. A foreman showed them through.

Juliet thought that what they saw was awful. And the smell was so terrible that most of the girls ran out.

"I never want to eat a piece of chicken again!" Pearl Keeler said afterward. Her face was as white as paper.

Some of the boys tried to act tough.

"It wasn't so bad," Lyle Turner said.

"Wasn't so bad! It was gross! All that blood and stuff."

"Well, you wouldn't want to eat a chicken that *hadn't* been killed, would you?" Joe asked her.

Mrs. White let them talk. Then she said, "Did you see those people who stood in a line? One of them did nothing but cut wings off. How would you like to do that every day for a living?"

"No!"

Then she said, "None of us would. But *somebody* has to clean chickens. I want you all to write a paper. Pretend that you work in that plant. Tell what it's like. What it smells like. And what it feels like."

"Why do you want us to do that?" Helen Boyd asked. "I want to forget the whole thing!"

"I want us to understand other people, Helen," Mrs. White said. "That's an important part of living. I want all of you to start trying to understand people who do different things than you do."

Juliet went home all excited. She had hated the plant. She felt so sorry for the people who had to work there. But she liked to write, and she worked hard on her paper.

But after it was finished, she thought, *This is too good! Mrs. White will wonder why my other papers have been so bad.* So she wrote it again, leaving out different things.

When Mrs. White read it, she sighed. "Your paper is all right, Juliet. But I thought that it would be better. I saw how the packing plant made you feel. I hoped you would put some of yourself into your writing."

"My spelling isn't too good," Juliet said.

"I don't mean that. Spelling is important, but even more important is to be able to put *truth* in writing."

"But I didn't tell any lies in my paper!"

"Of course not, Juliet." Mrs. White smiled. "But there are different forms of truth. For example, to say that 2 plus 2 is 4 is telling the truth. But to write about something you feel strongly about, so that you cause others to feel it, too—that's another kind of truth."

Juliet stared. She was thinking of the first paper she'd written. She wanted to get it and show it to Mrs. White. But instead she said, "I'll try harder next time."

What had happened to Helen Boyd's camera was still a mystery. And that bothered Juliet. The Boyds and the Rollinses kept on saying that Amos had stolen the camera. And they didn't like the Redfields coming to the meetings.

The other parents had welcomed the whole family. Mr. Redfield himself came to one meeting—in his wheelchair! Most everyone went out of his way to make both Mr. and Mrs. Redfield feel at home. The Redfields had come to church too—not the big church where the Rollinses went, but the small one the Joneses attended.

"The Boyds think they're so much better than anyone else," Juliet said to her mother. "Why don't they go find another group to be in?"

"They'd want to run that one too," Joe piped up. He scowled.

"That's enough of that sort of talk, both of you!" Mr. Jones had a frown on *his* face.

"I'm sorry, Dad." Joe ate another bite of pie, then said with his mouth full, "Anyway, I'm glad Amos and June are in our group."

"And they're learning fast," Mrs. Jones said. She had made several trips to the Redfield home to help the children with their writing. Debby Dubois went, too, to help with arithmetic.

"Amos may not be much good with books, but he's sure good in the woods," Joe said. "He knows the name of every plant and tree in the whole world."

"Maybe he could teach the rest of us," Juliet said. "I've tried to learn the kinds of trees from books, but it's hard."

"Yeah! We could have a field trip!" Joe's eyes got bright. "And we could cook out and all that stuff!"

"And I think that's a wonderful idea." Mrs.

Jones's eyes twinkled. "The fathers can take them and give the mothers a day off."

"Well, now, we'll just do that!" Mr. Jones said. "It'll be good for the guys too. I'll call them all—see if we can do it next Saturday."

First, though, Juliet and Joe went with their dad to clear the plan with the Redfields. She ran up to Amos and said very fast, "Amos! We're going on a field trip next Saturday! And you're going to teach us all about trees and stuff! And we're going to cook out! And—"

"Whoa!" Amos said. "Go slower. I can't—understand you!" He listened as she explained, but then he shook his head. "Can't—do it. The kids—would make fun of—the way I talk."

"When you go slow, you do all right," Juliet protested.

"No, some of them—don't like me. They won't listen."

"They will! My father is in charge," Juliet said. "And he'll jump on anyone who doesn't behave."

Finally Amos agreed.

Saturday morning, the home-school fathers and children all met at the small church. Mr. Rollins drove a van, and so did Mr. Turner.

Mr. Rollins took charge at once. "Get that food loaded!" he commanded.

"Who died and made him king?" Joe grumbled. But when he saw all the food, he was happy.

They parked the vans next to the woods and got out.

Mr. Rollins said, "Now we want you children to learn to recognize all the trees—and all the vines and bushes too." He walked over to a shiny green plant that was growing up the side of a tree. He looked at it carefully, then said in a loud voice, "Now, here is a wild berry vine."

"Let's check that with our vine expert," Mr. Jones said. He put his hand on Amos's shoulder and asked, "Is that a kind of wild berry vine, Amos?"

Amos shuffled his feet, then said, "No sir."

Mr. Rollins glared at him. "So what kind of a vine do you claim it is?"

"It's—poison ivy—Mr. Rollins."

Mr. Rollins turned pale. He went off and was seen washing his hands in a stream.

"So let's see how many trees we can learn to name," Mr. Jones said. "Amos, you're the teacher."

It was a hard moment for Amos, Juliet thought. He had never been known to say a word to the whole group at once. But she smiled at him.

Joe whispered, "Go for it, Amos!"

Amos swallowed, then pointed to a tree. "That's a—live oak. See that stuff—that looks like moss—in the branches?"

For the next hour they walked through the

woods. They made a game out of it. Amos would tell them the name of a tree or vine or wildflower. Then the others would try to find another one of the same kind. Pretty soon even the younger children could name some of the trees.

By the time they went back to the vans, everyone was hungry. They saw that some of the fathers had set up a grill and were cooking.

"Boy, smell those hamburgers!" Joe cried.

"Smells better than the chicken packing plant." Josie Keeler grinned.

The kids gulped down hamburgers as fast as the men could cook them. There was plenty of chips and dip too, not to mention gallons of lemonade.

After the picnic, Juliet's father said, "Let's sit down in the shade of that tree—"

"That's a sweet gum tree!" little Dani Dubois shouted. Everyone laughed, and Mr. Jones smiled at her. "You've learned a lot today, Dani. Amos, you're a good teacher!"

"He sure is!" Joe said. "I learned more about trees today than I ever learned in my whole life. I think we ought to study in the woods *all* the time!"

"It's easier to learn some things out of books, Joe. But right now all of you sit down. I'll read you a story while your lunch is settling." And he read part of the story of Joseph from the Bible. When he finished, he said, "Now, what do we learn from this wonderful story?"

Ray Boyd said, "If you try hard enough, you can get to be important. Joseph got to be the second most important man in all Egypt! He could do anything he wanted!"

But Jenny White shook her head. "Joseph didn't get to be important by himself. God helped him."

"And Joseph didn't get to be important just *for* himself," Mitch Dubois said. "He got to be important so he could help his brothers and other people when the famine came."

Ray didn't like to be wrong, so he kept arguing. But most of the others agreed with Jenny and Mitch.

Suddenly a new voice said, "I never heard that story. But I liked the way Joseph took care of his brothers when he had a chance. That's what you guys have done for Amos and me."

Everyone looked around. It was June Redfield. June had never before said a word in a group meeting! Even now she ducked her head.

Mr. Rollins looked displeased. "Your parents never read to you out of the Bible?" he demanded.

"They do now. My mother reads to us every night!" This time it was Amos speaking, and he didn't stutter a bit.

Mr. Jones jumped in. "That's fine, Amos. We're all glad to hear that. And you and June have done a lot for us, too. I think we've all learned how to better help others." Then he said, "And now, anyone ready for softball?"

A yell went up, and soon a game was underway. But it might have been better if they had gone home right after the Bible story.

Juliet was up at bat. She hit the ball over Helen Boyd's head. Helen was playing second base. Juliet went around first and saw Amos chasing the ball. But she thought she could make it to second. She ran as hard as she could.

Helen was yelling, "Throw me the ball! Throw me the ball!"

Amos picked up the ball and saw that Juliet was headed for second base. He threw very hard. The ball went right between Helen's hands and hit her in the stomach. She fell over. But she jumped up at once. Her face was red, and she began screaming, "You did that on purpose!"

Amos was trying to say he was sorry, but Ray Boyd ran up and hit him in the face. Amos didn't hit back. He just started backing away, still trying to apologize.

Then Helen ran at him and hit him in the face, too. She shouted, "You big dummy! You're so stupid you can't do anything right!"

And that's when Juliet lost it all!

She rushed at Helen. She drew back her fist and hit her on the nose! Helen began screaming. Then she grabbed Juliet by the hair. That hurt, so Juliet grabbed Helen's hair. They fell to the ground, still pulling hair and shouting.

The fathers pulled them apart. Mr. Boyd started shouting about what one bad kid could do to a bunch of good kids. But Juliet's father said, "Let's go home. We'll talk about it later."

All the way back to town, Juliet didn't say a word. She was sitting between Amos and Joe. Just before they got home, a tear trickled down her cheek. What she'd done was wrong. She would have to apologize to Helen—and to Jesus.

She tried hard not to cry, but she couldn't help it. She let the tears flow. Then she felt something nudge her side. She looked down. Amos was offering her a handkerchief.

She saw that he was doing his best to make her feel better. She took it and wiped her face. Then she handed it back.

"Thank you, Amos," she whispered.

He whispered, "Thank you, Juliet." He paused for a long time. Then he said softly with a big smile, "You're my friend, Juliet!"

10

Juliet Quits

But I couldn't help it, Dad!"

Juliet's father had asked her to go for a walk before supper. As soon as they were away from the house, he brought up her fight with Helen.

"It was *her* fault! You heard those names she called Amos!"

"Yes, I did. And she was wrong. But that's *her* problem, Juliet. We can't help what other people do. But we *can* do something about our own acts."

The afternoon sun was streaming through the trees as they walked along. They were elm trees, Juliet noticed. She remembered that Amos had taught her to recognize them. And as she thought of Amos, she grew angry at Helen again. She loved her father, and she knew

Mrs. White looked at Juliet's mother. "About Juliet?"

"Yes. I'm very concerned about her."

"So am I." Mrs. White took a sip of coffee, then put down the cup. "She's obviously not doing her best with the team. Do you know why?"

"I have an idea, but it may not be right. All her father and I know for sure is that she's not happy. For one thing, she's never really forgiven Helen Boyd for what she said about Amos."

Vicki looked toward the stairs. "Here they come. I'll try to talk to Juliet about it sometime today."

All the way to the church, Joe chattered like a squirrel. He was more excited about the Home School Bowl than Juliet had expected. "Hey, Mrs. White," he said as they got out of the car at the church. "I think we're a cinch to win, don't you?"

"It depends on how the team does, Joe," she said. "A lot of things go to make up a team. Everyone has to do his best. It's like a car. No matter how good the engine is, if just *one thing* doesn't work, the car doesn't go anywhere."

They entered the meeting room and found most of the other students there. Juliet went over to Amos and June at once and said, "Hi. How are things at your house?"

"Great!" Amos grinned. "Dad is going to—

start using his cane next week. Pretty soon—he'll go—back to work."

"I think that's grand!" Juliet said.

"All right," Mrs. White said loudly. "This will be a run-through." She held up some envelopes. "These are questions that have been used in past years. They won't be used this year, but some like them will."

"I'd like to see *this* year's questions!" Billy Rollins said.

"If you know your stuff, Billy," Mrs. White said, "you don't need to see them. Now, get into your seats, and we'll begin. First, we'll review spelling."

It was the worst team meeting Juliet had ever been to. Some kids seemed to have forgotten everything they knew. As Mrs. White reviewed, Juliet wanted to shout out the answers time and again. But when her turn came, she forced herself to miss a lot of the questions.

"Good night!" Lyle Turner groaned. "We're getting *worse,* not better!"

"Maybe we better not even go this year," Mary Rose Turner said nervously. "It'd be awful to get there and do as bad as this!"

But Ray shouted, "No! We're going to win!"

"How do you expect to win with the dead weight we're carrying?" Billy Rollins said that. He didn't mention any names, but he was glaring at Amos. He gave Juliet a look, too. Then he said, "I think we ought to have some kind of elimination. If any kid doesn't come up with good stuff, don't let him go to the contest!"

He got a little support from Jack Turner and Helen Boyd. But most of the students shouted him down.

"It's all of us or none of us!" Joe said loudly.

"Boys and girls, we can't argue like this," Mrs. White interrupted. "I want you all to pray every day for the other members of the team. I'm sure you're already praying for yourselves, but it's important to remember others too."

As she went on talking, Juliet felt worse and worse. She knew that her feelings about Helen Boyd were wrong. But she couldn't seem to change them. When it was time for refreshments and games, she forced herself to smile at Helen. "You have such a pretty dress on, Helen," she said. "Is it new?"

Helen said, "Yes." Then she walked away and left Juliet standing alone, feeling angry again.

Mary Rose and Jenny had seen it all. Mary Rose said, "Come on, Juliet. You can be our partner in the next game."

Juliet was happy that they were nice to her. But she still was angry.

Then it was time to leave, and Billy Rollins said, "Hey, where's my new pen? It was right here with my stuff." He started looking through his books and papers. "It's not here."

And he looked right at Amos. "I'll bet *you* took it—just like you did the camera!"

Amos just stood staring at him.

And then Juliet really lost her temper again. She was already angry at Helen, and this was too much. "He didn't take your old pen!" she cried.

Billy Rollins started to yell something.

But Juliet screamed at him. "You're nothing but a bully! You think you're better than anybody else!"

Billy yelled back at her. He reached out and gave her a push. Juliet staggered back. Joe came running at Billy. He shoved Billy, and Billy went down on the floor.

Mrs. White cried out, "Stop that! All of you!" She got in the middle of it and began to tell them how badly they were behaving.

As she was talking, Helen Boyd stuck out her tongue at Juliet.

Juliet suddenly said, "I won't be in this old contest! I quit!"

Mrs. White said, "Now, Juliet, that's no way to act!"

Juliet Jones screwed up her face to keep the tears back. She ignored the pleading looks of Amos and June. She shook off Joe, who was pulling at her arm and saying, "Aw, come on, Juliet!"

She walked out of the building and got into Mrs. White's car. Joe came out and tried to talk to her, but she said, "No! I'm not going to be in that silly old contest!"

When Juliet got home, she went right to her room and threw herself on her bed. She knew her mother would come in as soon as Mrs. White told her what had happened. But Juliet didn't care.

She'd had enough of Billy Rollins and the Boyds!

11

The Trap

For more than a week Juliet kept her mouth shut tight. Her parents and Mrs. White tried to talk to her. She just shook her head. The other children tried to get her to come back to the team. She wouldn't even argue.

But every day she was miserable. It was one of those times people have when they *know* they're behaving badly but won't change their ways.

Amos Redfield came to her house one day and knocked on the door. Mrs. Jones went to see who it was. "Why, Amos," she said, "how nice to see you! Come on inside."

Amos swallowed hard but shook his head. "I'd like—to see Juliet."

Mrs. Jones saw that he was very serious. She said gently, "Of course, Amos. I'll get her."

She left him standing at the door and went to Juliet's room.

"It's Amos," she said. "He wants to see you." As Juliet got up from the desk, her mother added, "He looks worried."

"Maybe something's happened at home. I'll find out."

She went downstairs and out onto the porch. "Hello, Amos," she said. "Is somebody sick at your house?"

"No," he said. "Will you go for—a walk with me?"

"Walk with you? Why, sure. Let me tell Mom where I'm going."

Soon the two of them were heading down the street. It was still early morning. A cool breeze was coming off the hills.

For a while, Amos said little. He pointed out a pair of fox squirrels in a tall oak. "Nothing better than—squirrel and dumplings!"

"They're so cute, though," Juliet said. "I'd hate to eat them."

They walked on. Finally she asked, "What's wrong, Amos? I know something is."

He said, "Let's sit—on that big rock." They sat down, and he said, "It's not anything—wrong with me. It's you—I'm worried about."

"Me? What about me?"

"Well, you quit the team. It makes me sad. And June too."

"I did it because those old Boyds and Billy Rollins were so mean to you," she said quickly.

"It didn't—bother me that much," he said. "I don't expect—much out of them. But I don't—like to see you—act like this." He had a hard time putting things into words, as usual. "Me and June—we been listening to—the Bible stories. I thought—Christians were supposed—to forgive people."

"They are!"

"Then, why—don't you stop—being mad at the Boyds and Billy?"

Juliet felt her cheeks turn red. She knew he was right. Suddenly she began to cry. "I don't know why I've acted so crazy!" she whispered.

He seemed embarrassed by her tears. "Well, I just—wanted you to know me and June—well, whatever you do—we'll always like you!"

He got up and walked off.

Juliet sat on the big rock for a long time. Then she got up and walked toward her house. When she was halfway there, Joe met her. "What's wrong?" he asked. "Why are you crying?"

"Oh, Joe," she moaned. "I've been so icky!"

"You sure have," he agreed. "I've been telling you that."

"What made me do such a thing?"

"I don't know. Maybe you really *are* dumb," he said with a grin. "Maybe you pretended to be dumb so long, you just got dumb." But he put his arm around her. "I'm just kidding. Are you going to come back to the team?"

Juliet was thinking hard. "The kids called me Too Smart Jones. Well, I've not acted very smart. But I've got an idea that might be a *little* smart. I think it'll solve the mystery of the missing camera."

When she had told Joe her plan, he shouted, "I better call you Too Smart myself! That's a great plan! When do we try it?"

"Tomorrow night," Juliet said. "It's the big Sleep-in at the church. Help me get everything ready!"

The Sleep-in was one of the most fun things the team got to do. Every year, a few days before the Home School Bowl, they all met at the church with two sets of parents. Everybody brought blankets and bedrolls and lots of snacks. They stayed up as late as they wanted. Some always bragged that they would stay up all night, but nobody ever did.

The team members were surprised to see Juliet.

"Are you back on the team?" Josie Keeler asked.

"I just came for the Sleep-in," Juliet said. She noticed that most of the kids seemed glad to see her. She joined in the games and tried to be nice to everyone.

She had brought along something special

for Show-and-Tell time. "This is my new gyroscope," she said. "I saved up for three months for it. This is how it works . . ."

The stainless steel gyroscope was a series of steel circles that looked like a ball. Right through the middle of it was a steel rod. The rod that came out the bottom had a slot in it. Juliet wound a string around the gyroscope, and when she pulled the string hard, one of the circles started spinning.

"Now, Joe, hold out *your* string," Juliet said.

Joe held a piece of string at the ends, and Juliet rested the slotted end of the rod on his string. "Now watch," she said. She took her hands away from the gyroscope, and it balanced on the string!

"What keeps it from falling off?" Dani Dubois asked.

"That's nothing!" Juliet said. "Look at this!" She put her hand on the gyroscope and moved it. Now it was not on top of the string. It stuck out to one side! It still just hung on there, not falling!

Ray Boyd's eyes were big as saucers. "Why doesn't it fall off?"

"It's because of centrifugal force," Juliet said. "But don't ask me what that is. I don't know. I do know they use these things in the rockets they send to the moon."

The gyroscope was the hit of Show and

hands glowing. They must belong to whoever took the gyroscope."

"It's that Redfield boy!" Mr. Boyd said. "We've got him this time!" And then he turned on the lights.

Most everybody gave a little cry of surprise. Even Mr. Boyd.

He cried out, "Ray! What have you done!"

Someone was staring at his hands, but it was not Amos. It was Ray Boyd. He tried to hide his hands. Then he saw everyone looking at him. "It was just a joke!"

"Not much of a joke, Ray," Mr. Turner said. "Did you take Helen's camera too?"

"I just wanted to use it for a little while," Ray said. He was very pale, and his voice shook. "She wouldn't ever let me use it, so I took it."

"And you let Amos take the blame!" Mr. Turner looked very stern. "I'm afraid this is very serious, Ray. It means that *you* can't go with the team to the Home School Bowl."

Ray's father looked as if he was going to be sick. He walked to Ray and put his hand out. "Come on, Son. Let's go home."

When all the Boyds were gone, Mr. Turner said, "I know you kids will all pray for Ray. He needs your prayers very much."

Juliet said, "I—I will."

"That's fine, Juliet!" Mrs. Turner said. "Why don't we all just pray right now?"

As they prayed, Juliet found herself praying not only for Ray but for Helen and for Billy Rollins. Most of all she prayed for herself. And when they were finished, she was smiling. She felt good for the first time in weeks!

"Hey, Juliet," Josie asked. "How'd you figure out how to do all that smart stuff? With the gyroscope, I mean."

"Yes," her sister Pearl said. "I thought you weren't very smart."

And now everyone was staring at Juliet.

"I think you're smarter than you've been acting," Lyle Turner said.

"Maybe she's *too* smart," Joe said with a grin.

"You be quiet!" Juliet said quickly before he could say more.

"Well, somebody had better get smart," Mr. Turner said. He rubbed his chin hard. He looked around at the boys and girls. "The Oakwood team has just lost its star math student. Without Ray, we're in trouble."

Joe looked up at the ceiling. Then he said, "You never can tell, Mr. Turner. Before the Home School Bowl is over, some of us might get a whole lot smarter than you'd ever believe!"

She had on a new blue dress. She and her mother had picked it out just for the Home School Bowl. It had a full skirt with a hoop that made it stand out. And she and Jenny had made a visit to the beauty shop—their first time to go! But with all that, Juliet wasn't excited. She just sat as her family kept on talking.

"Did you know Amos and June went by to visit Ray?" her dad asked. "That made quite an impression on the Boyds. Mr. Boyd told me he'd been about ready to move to another town. But he said people had been so kind when Ray had his trouble. And that changed his mind. I think the Boyds will be different people now."

"It's taught us all something," Mrs. Jones said. Then she looked ahead. "Well, here we are at Cedar City. We're going to be just on time."

They parked in the large lot beside the huge church. Juliet saw that all the other members of the Oakwood support group were already there. She got out and at once was surrounded by excited boys and girls.

"We're going to win this thing!" Billy Rollins boasted. "I stayed up and studied all night."

Amos was there. And June. And there was his father—standing with the help of two canes. He gave Juliet and Joe a wink. "How about this?" He smiled. "Never thought I'd see my kids in a contest like this!"

Jenny grabbed Juliet's hand. "Oh, I'm so nervous!" she said. "I—I wish I'd worked harder."

"You'll do fine, Jenny," Juliet said. She squeezed the smaller girl's hand.

Then Mrs. White called, "It's time to go for it. But first, once again let's ask God to give us clear minds."

"Let's ask Him to let us win!" Billy said.

"No, we won't pray that," Mrs. White said. She looked around the circle. She was smiling, but at the same time Juliet could tell that she was serious. "This is only a contest. It doesn't really matter who gets first place. What matters is that we've learned so much. And not just about math and writing and science," she said. "We've learned a lot about working together. And about understanding each other."

Ray Boyd said, "*I* sure have!" he said. "I guess I've learned more than anybody. I learned how crazy it is to take other people's things. And I learned how nice some people can be when a fellow is in trouble!"

"Hooray for Ray!" Amos shouted, and they all gave a cheer.

Then Ray said, "I'm sure sorry I won't be able to help the team. But I'll be with you next year."

"That's a good attitude, Ray," Mrs. White said. "Now let's ask the Lord Jesus to help us do our best. And to give us joy in their victory if the other team wins. After all, the Cedar City people are our friends. And we want to see our friends do well. Even if it costs us something we want."

She bowed her head and began to pray, but Juliet didn't hear a word. She was thinking of what she'd just heard: *We want to see our friends do well. Even if it costs us something we want.*

Suddenly she understood that the words were for her.

I've been worrying so much about an old nickname that I've been letting my friends down!

She silently prayed that God would help her do what she now knew she had to do.

Many people were gathered inside the church. Most of them were from Cedar City. But she also saw visitors from Oakwood. A yell went up as they came in, and there was the pastor of their church on his feet.

"Looks like Brother Stone brought the whole church with him!" Joe said to Juliet.

Up front, two men and three women were seated at a table. To their right was the Cedar City team. Across from them were some empty chairs draped with blue ribbons.

"That's where we sit," Mrs. White said.

Juliet sat down between Josie and Helen.

"I'm scared stiff!" Josie mumbled.

"Me too!" Helen whispered.

Juliet took a deep breath. Then she said, loudly enough for the whole team to hear her, "Don't anyone be afraid. Just do your best!"

Billy Rollins had left all his bragging outside. He was so nervous he could hardly talk. "I wish I'd worked harder!" he groaned. "I wish I was dead!"

Then the contest began.

A lady stood and said, "Welcome to the annual Home School Bowl. I am Mrs. Taylor. The five judges you see here are all either teachers now or have been. None of us has any connection with either team. We are determined to be absolutely fair to everyone. Mr. Derek Blackmon is a science teacher from a local high school. He will direct the science quiz. Mr. Blackmon, will you begin?"

Mr. Blackmon was a thin man with bright blue eyes. "If those students who are to compete in science will come forward, we will get started."

"Oh, boy!" Jack Turner groaned. "I sure wish Ray was here!"

Suddenly Juliet left her seat and went to stand beside Lyle Turner and Roy Keeler. They stared at her. Mrs. White stared at her. The whole Oakwood team stared at her. Juliet looked at Mrs. White. She was ready to sit down if Mrs. White said so. But then Mrs. White smiled and nodded.

Mr. Blackmon started the quiz, and it was hard! The students from Cedar City were good. But so were Lyle and Roy. Science wasn't Juliet's best subject. Still, she was able to help the two boys pull up the Oakwood score.

When the science part was over, Mr. Blackmon said, "If you will take your seats, the judges will total up the scores and announce the winner at once."

Juliet's legs were a little weak as she made her way to her seat. Billy Rollins grabbed her arm as she passed him. "How come you knew all that stuff?"

She just shrugged and sat down. She looked across the room at her parents. Both of them were smiling. Her father held up two fingers in a V for Victory sign.

"The scores are very close," Mrs. Taylor announced. "For Oakwood, 117 points. And for Cedar City, 134 points."

A yell went up from the Cedar City people.

Mrs. White said quietly to the team, "That's fine. It's much better than anyone thought we'd do in science."

The next contest was spelling. Lynn Turner and Mitch Dubois led the Oakwood team. When the scores were announced, it was 126 points for Oakwood and 117 points for Cedar City. This time it was the Oakwood supporters who did the cheering.

The contest went on. Then there came a break. Each team went to its own special room for break time. There were soft drinks and milk, plus a few cookies.

"Don't overdo on those," Mrs. White warned. "We've still got two hours to go."

"We're 45 points behind," Billy Rollins complained. "We'll never win!"

"Don't lose your confidence," Mrs. White said. "And no matter if we win or lose, I'm proud of you."

Helen Boyd suddenly spoke up. She was looking at Juliet in a strange way. "Juliet," she asked, "what's happened to you? You're different!"

"Yeah," Billy Rollins put in. "How'd you get so smart in one day? Yesterday you were dumb. Today you're smart. You taking some kind of *smart* pill?"

Juliet knew it was time. She took a deep breath and said, "I have to confess something . . ."

She started at the beginning and told the whole story. She'd pretended not to be smart, because of the way it had been in the town they came from. She told them about the name "Too Smart Jones." She told them how she hadn't had many friends.

"I've learned that most of that was my own fault," she said. She swallowed hard. "I—I know I was proud of being smart. And I looked down on kids who didn't make as good grades."

It got very quiet in the room.

"I've learned that I was wrong. Jesus made us all different. I can spell better than some, but some can add better than I can. And some people can't add *or* spell very well. But they're kind. And maybe that's the best thing of all."

"It sure is!" Amos said. He looked very nice in his new clothes. "I'm not—going to call you —Too Smart Jones," he said with a grin. "Know what I'm—going to call you?"

"What?" Juliet asked, dreading another nickname.

"I'm going to call you Too Nice Jones."

A laugh went up, and Juliet cried, "You'd better not, Amos Redfield! I'll crown you if you call me that!"

"Don't worry, Juliet," Joe assured her. "When Amos knows you as well as *I* do, he'll call you Clumsy Jones!"

Mrs. White held up her hand to stop the laughter. "Well, we're glad to have the new Juliet Jones with us today. But now it's time to go back for the last part of the contest. And remember, win or lose, we're going to be content!"

The two teams stayed tied all morning. For a time Cedar City would lead. Then Oakwood would pass them.

Finally Mrs. Taylor stood up. "So far, the score is Cedar City 865 points and Oakwood 845 points."

Nobody cheered much, for it was a tense moment.

She said, "As you know, there is one more

contest—the art competition. This will decide the winner of the annual Home School Bowl. The judges will now go to the room where the artwork is on display."

As the judges got up, Amos's father hobbled forward on his canes. He managed to hold a large paper sack in his hand at the same time. "Is it too late to put something in the show for Oakwood?" he asked.

"Not at all." Mrs. Taylor took the sack, looked in, and went into the display room with the judges.

"Nothing to do now but wait," Joe said. He looked glum. "We're goners. I saw some of the art these kids from Cedar City did. "They are *really* good!"

"It's not over till it's over," Mitch Dubois said. Then he asked, "Amos, what was in the sack your dad gave Mrs. Taylor?"

"Oh, just some—stuff I did," Amos said. "It's not very good."

The team waited nervously. After a long time, the judges came back and sat down. Mrs. Taylor had a paper in her hand.

"The art competition is one of the most difficult of all to judge," she said. "It's easy to know when an addition problem is incorrect. But painting and other art is not as simple."

It got very quiet as she looked at the paper in her hand. "The judges, however, agree. The Cedar City art won a total of 183 points. That brings their total to 1,048." She looked up, then said, "The art of the Oakwood team was worth 186 points—"

One of Cedar City's math team cried out, "Then we win!"

"Wait! That's not all!" Mrs. Taylor said. "You know that the best art on display brings an extra 50 points. The judges agree that the carvings submitted by Amos Redfield are the best works of art in the entire collection. Therefore, the winner of this year's Home School Bowl, with a total of 1,081 points, is Oakwood!"

When the cheering stopped, Mrs. Taylor had more to say. "We believe that there is no loser in this contest today. Both teams have done well. We are proud of every single one of you!"

Then it was over. Juliet ran over to Amos. But Mr. Rollins was ahead of her. He was shaking Amos's hand. "I always knew this boy had talent!" he was saying. "And I hear that you need a set of carving tools. Well, I intend to buy the best set on the market for you, young man!"

Joe groaned. "Mr. Rollins takes all the credit for everything!"

Juliet finally got to Amos. "Oh, Amos, I'm so proud of you!"

"Maybe—they'll be calling me—Too Smart Amos now!" He was grinning. "But I don't care

—how smart you are, Juliet. You're my friend. The best—I ever had!"

"You have lots of friends, Amos," Juliet said.

Then Joe came up. He slapped Amos on the back. "Next year we'll show this bunch. I'm going to invent a machine that never runs down. That'll win some points."

Juliet laughed. "You're the one who never runs down!" Then she took each of them by the arm and said, "Dad's buying a victory lunch for the winners."

"I hope the hamburgers have mustard!" Joe said hungrily. "I always hated mayonnaise!"